DEDICATION

This book is dedicated to all our journeys through life;
that it might help encourage introspection.

ACKNOWLEDGMENTS

To my elder brother and his wife: thank you for helping
me complete this journey to self-publishing. It was a
long road; one you helped make smoother.

To my mother: for her willingness to serve as both my
editor *and* proofreader... over and over again; as I wrote
and rewrote this story until, <u>finally</u>, it is **better** than I
ever could have imagined.

CONTENTS

"Death is but a facade upon existence."

rologue

Silver elevator doors sat motionless; a little out of place in the austere setting of a sterile hospital corridor. The current floor number displayed above these shiny doors, abruptly switched from one to two.

Just down the hall could be seen a pair of worn white sneakers, squeaking with each slight shift of their owners legs, propped atop the curved oval of a green nurse's desk.

Some ten seconds later - as the faint arrival chime sounded, the overhead golden indicator light blinked to three, and the doors began to slide open - a slim hand, firmly clutching a scrap of wrinkled note paper, thrust through the widening gap, pushing in vain on the slowly recessing twin doors.

Just *before* the elevator's chime, the shoes on the desk hurriedly slid from sight.

A slim woman darted from the elevator, her thin frame turning sideways to fit through the widening gap. Glancing from the piece of paper in her hand, then to the black guiding arrows on the wall, she hastened down the pallid corridor in a dark blue ankle-length skirt, her heels clicking loudly on the reflective concrete. Stumbling on the polished floor, she yelped in pain—her ankle twisting beneath her.

Catching herself on the far wall, she pulled off the offending footwear -- and, shoes dangling from her hand, the young woman - now limping slightly on stockinged feet – hurried her way past the third floor nurse's station.

"Can I help you find the room?" Though startled, she spared only a quick glance and head shake for the intent male nurse, who stood expectantly behind his desk. "No, I'm good." Scrutinizing the note clutched in her hand, the tall man nodded, settling back down into his chair. Watching her pass out of sight down the corridor, he checked his watch, nodding in satisfaction.

The young woman, already three doors beyond the desk, jogged on at a near run, silently mouthing each of the growing room numbers; "353, 354, 355..." She stopped abruptly in front of a metal door typical to this corridor, her swaying blond braid coming to rest over one shoulder. Inset just above the doorknob was a narrow viewing window. Peering through the glass, her pale eyebrows - almost invisible against last summer's tan - creased with worry. Two of her uncles, their wives, plus some of their older children, stood conversing near the room's center, their subdued voices nearly inaudible from the hall.

Reaching for the knob, she took in a shuddering

breath… The tremor was not one of exhaustion, nor was it caused by the cool metal beneath her fingers. Shoes clutched tightly in her hand like a weapon, she squared her shoulders and pushed open the door, stepping determinedly into the hospital room.

Glancing over as she entered, her uncle, John, broke off, but she'd heard the first of his sullen words from the corridor. "I don't know why we even bothered coming. *He* never wanted…"

His harsh tone left her with no doubts… His estranged father was already dead to him, despite the hospital monitors, which still continued their steady, plaintive beeps.

Following John's lead, no one spoke; all refusing

eye contact with her. The scattering of children in the room, who sat either dozing in plastic chairs along the wall, or coloring quietly, copied their elders, watching her covertly.

Looking towards her grandfather's hospital bed, she saw to her disgust not one of them was sitting near. They didn't acknowledge her presence as she walked past their chairs, approaching her grandfather's supine form. There, upon an elevated hospital mattress he lay, the shallow rise and fall of his chest nearly imperceptible. She looked down tenderly on the white haired man, her somber blue eyes prickling with tears.

Her shoes clattering to the floor, she reached down to clasp his hand; the beds rounded railing pressing hard against her hips. This shrunken shell before her was nothing like the energetic friend she had played with as a girl -- the robust man she had always loved and respected.

Her breath caught, as his eyelids briefly flickered. Bending in close, she clasped his once large, but now withered hand between hers. No further movement showed beneath his wrinkled lids. His fingers twitched under her hands; then, with a final sigh of air from his sunken lips, she felt his body grow still. "He's... gone." Her voice quavered.

"Are you sure..." Her uncle's question was both drowned out and answered by the sudden shriek of life support. Susan stood there numbly as all the children covered their ears. The two youngest woke in fright, and ran to hug their mothers' legs.

The nurse from down the hall arrived at a jog. Yanking open the door he hurried to the bed. Everyone scattered, then filtered wordlessly from the room, leaving Susan alone with her grief. The nurse, working around her, gently took the IV needle from his arm. Next he shut off the shrill alarm, bringing a deathly quiet to the room. Paying no heed, Susan still clutched her grandfather's lifeless hand.

Closing her eyes, head lowered, Susan remembered the times she had spent with her grandfather -- the occasions he had taken her up in his chopper as his co-pilot, helped her complete her college essays, or sat discussing anything and everything under the sun; their talking points ranging from the shy boy in two of her classes, who kept glancing at her, but had yet to ask her out, to the more intimidating aspect of becoming his financial heiress. She recalled her last goodbye to him there on the beach -- his forlorn expression as she had gotten into her car to drive away last summer - his lonely figure shrinking away in her rear view mirror -- and her tears began to flow in earnest.

She bent to kiss his forehead, tears falling on his white hair. "I'll miss you so much, you stubborn, wonderful man."

From behind her, a pair of strong arms wrapped about her waist. "I'm so sorry I didn't get here in time." Turning around in his arms, she embraced her husband. "Oh Mark" she sobbed, "he's gone." Stroking her hair, he spoke soothingly. "Come on Suzie, there's nothing more we can do; let's go home."

Wordlessly, the nurse watched them depart, before turning his attention back to his task, preparing the body for its final destination.

CHAPTER 1

As the gauntlet of death closed around his mind, Greg floated placidly amongst fading memories…, dreaming of happier days; the night his eldest son was born, the moment he signed his first company loan, and the first time he had thrown his giggling granddaughter Suzie into the air.

At first he thought it only a memory as he felt her warm hands gripping his, but with a familiar squeeze of her fingers - the way she had of tightly clasping his hands when greeting him - he knew it must be real.

His stroke damaged brain would not deny him this last chance of saying goodbye! He fought for consciousness. For an instant his fingers responded, flexing weakly around Susan's hand.

Then, panic gripping his thoughts, he felt some intrinsic part of himself - never before noticed - slip free of his tired old body. This inner self became his whole existence. Now the only sensation he felt was darkness, and directionless movement.

A bright light appeared ahead, approaching quickly, its illumination revealing his plummet down a tunnel of natural stone.

Greg had never been a believer, and so he found this light beyond the darkness of death's embrace, very surprising.

But as the light swelled, threatening to blot out his vision, his velocity gradually slowed, then halted. He threw up an arm to block his face from the dazzling brilliance, and discovering that he again had a body, he turned and ran from what he instinctively knew to be the light of permanent death. Glancing back from his hurried progress into the darkness, he saw the glow was nearer! Finally, panting and exhausted, thoroughly frustrated from his desire to say goodbye to Susan, he faced about and was drawn into the radiance.

Greg stepped out through an arch in the stone, the bright light beyond, quickly fading away; leaving behind a dimly lit, mist blanketed scene. His first cautious step from the cave, immediately brought to his attention the gritty feel of rounded pebbles beneath his naked feet. The disturbed grey surface of a pea gravel path, stretching out before him, was sunken in spots, and elevated in others, by what seemed a multitude of passing feet.

Stepping further from the cave… into one of these multitudinous footprints, he found his own foot size and shape to be a perfect match, right down to the slight splaying of his middle toes! Greg felt certain he had never been here before, yet the print's match was far too perfect to be a coincidence.

As he passed fully through the threshold of the cave's mouth, Greg sensed more than felt an invisible barrier spring into existence behind him. Reaching back towards the entrance... sure enough, Greg discovered a strong resistance in the seemingly empty air - repelling his hand. It must be some kind of ward - preventing reentry to his old life. Turning to face the empty air, he threw a punch at the... force field? Success! His fist and arm penetrated some two feet into the cave mouth, but it felt like he had hit a rubber wall. His eyes widened in surprise as the flux barrier sprang back into shape. His arm was violently deflected, sending him into a spin. Tripping clumsily over his own feet, he ended up sprawling face-first in the gravel, his shoulder aching from the wrench it had received.

Greg scrambled to his feet, glaring at the cave as he dusted himself off. …Not that he had much to dust. The gravel was - quite naturally - wet, leaving beads of moisture clinging to his bare torso... running down his skin like a mourner's tears. It seemed he was trapped here. Wherever here was.

Cupping his hands, he shouted out, "Hellooo!" His unfamiliar voice was instantly swallowed by the thin air, not the faintest echo returning to him.

Just ahead, first vanishing, then reappearing through drifting trailers of fog, Greg could faintly make out a trail marker. He walked forward, curious to find out more about this place. With every step, rocks ground loudly beneath his soles; yet he felt no discomfort.

As he neared the greying post of rough-cut timber, a path was revealed through the mist, running far into the distance on his left - but to his right - disappearing quickly into dense fog. This sign post seemed to serve as a divisional line in the path - for while the misted trail to his right was rough, climbing steeply upward, the paved way to his left widened out invitingly, sloping gently downward; not enough to tire a traveler's calves, but just enough to ease the way. It seemed to meander almost playfully among flower beds and well-tended grass, but on the horizon hung a red-ringed sun - glaring through the mist. The sight was ominous indeed, and Greg looked away with a shudder.

Peering up at the long weathered plank serving as a duo-directional sign, Greg studied the inscriptions placed on either end—seeming to have been written in an ancient text; but from one blink to the next they distorted, morphing into English.

The words on the left side of the marker - seemed to have been stamped upon the grayed timber with a hot brand. 'THE VOID'. This short description only made his shivering worsen—his sparsely clothed body exposed to the chill air. That did not seem like a place he could find peace...; mayhap, oblivion? Still... the way to his left looked warm and inviting…

In contrast, the right hand marker was inscribed
with obvious care, bearing the words "Cloud City",
in a pleasant if flowery indented script. Looking left
then right, Greg stepped forward, making his
choice.

CHAPTER 2

Greg made quick progress up a boulder-tumbled slope; in the utter silence, his labored breathing sounding loud in his ears—even the occasional clatter of dislodged stones, strangely muffled in the saturated air.

Despite the moist chill, the hard work of scaling some of the larger boulders blocking the path, soon had perspiration dripping from his brow.

Raising a hand to wipe sweat from his eyes, Greg

traced calloused fingers over the unfamiliar features of his face—down to his too small nose and overly full lips; along a jawline a little sharper than it ought to be; then up to his ear—a bit less protuberant than before. Despite these alterations to his looks, something about this new body felt disconcertingly familiar.

So fixated was he on the puzzle of his new identity, Greg forgot to look where he was stepping—not noticing the small chunk of stone directly in his path. Sharp pain jolted through his foot, yanking him back to the present. It felt like an anvil had just dropped on it! Cursing in agony, Greg leaned up against a nearby boulder, lifting his dusty foot to inspect the damage. He was astonished to see he'd suffered no major injury. He wasn't even cut. A series of scarred calluses along his toes had protected him.

Greg stared uncertainly at the series of long healed abrasions; his shivers returning, even as the pain - so sharp at first - began to ebb. "Better keep moving before I freeze to... what, life?"

Soon the uncertain terrain and slick boulders were not all Greg had to contend with - for growing close along the path were wicked thorns—capable of lacerating his skin with a single touch. In fact, here and there, a thorn's tip was dyed a reddish brown; proving others had passed this way. They had not been as careful as he.

No sooner did he think this, than he was gritting his teeth in pain. Greg clutched at his shoulder, a single careless movement, resulting in a thorn slicing his skin. The cut was shallow——but much as stubbing his toes had been, it hurt inordinately! He trudged onward, aware of how the vines left just enough room to pass - if he was careful.

When Greg felt he couldn't go on without a rest - the path leveled off. To his relief, the thorn bushes also retreated. Soon they gave way altogether, replaced by a jumbled field of broken stone.

Placing his hands on his knees, Greg sat atop a flat boulder to rest. Avoiding all those thorns had made his progress slow.

Though thoroughly exhausted—he was surprised how quickly his strength returned. In less than a minute he felt capable of setting out again.

The path was now clear, though boulders were heaped to either side of the trail—ominous in the shrouding mist.

Towering monoliths loomed… Juts and angles in the stone, like craggy faces, peered down at him. Their oppressive shadow seemed to swallow all sound.

Behind and to the sides, they seemed to lean in, threatening to topple if ignored too long. He refused to be intimidated—looking straight ahead... Nothing happened.

Grinning triumphantly, he walked confidently down the path.

It was more a disturbance of the air, than a sound from behind that alerted him to the mass of shifting stone. Glancing behind, the path was gone—a solid wall of boulders blocking his retreat.

With a little less confidence in his step, Greg picked up the pace. Glancing behind—the wall seemed to be stalking him—but while under observance, held perfectly still.

Thinking to outsmart it, he looked backwards

while walking, and it soon faded into the shroud.

Greg's knee suddenly collided against rock! As he reeled back, there, in front of him, towered the familiar wall of lowering stone! He turned to flee, yet there it was again_behind him! With nowhere left to go, Greg waited for the trap to close; for the boulders to converge! Not that he was going to go down without a fight! Bracing his back against the uneven stone surface, Greg prepared to face his impending doom. But no, through the drifting trailers of mist, Greg perceived that once again the way was clear.

Confused and frightened, Greg took off running, not daring to look behind or to the sides.

The cold air soon had his lungs burning, forcing Greg to slow. The mist was gradually thinning; unmuted day finally encroaching and warming the air—the boulders - once so frightening in the half-light - steadily becoming less jagged, diminishing in size.

Between one step and the next, a rhythmic pulsing thrum became audible. What did it remind him of…? It was a slow and steady heartbeat, coupled with close breathing. The sound recalled a memory; the feeling of being surrounded by cherishing protection. Greg hesitated - eyes shut…to conceive a time before thoughts were shaped by words. With a single blind step forward,

the sound was again a fading memory.

CHAPTER 3

Cracking his lids, Greg squinted against the warming brightness of a sanguine sun. Stretched out before him lay his pallid shadow; its elongated legs reaching far down a sparkling white sidewalk. Yet despite the sun's determined brightness - his shadow lacked density—its edges dull.

Glancing behind, Greg saw no sign of the obstacles he had overcome—only a long stretch of downward sloping concrete--separating him from the signpost—marking the inroad from which he had entered this illusionary world. Beyond that lay the path of ease… Yet in comparison to where Greg now stood, the sunlight there seemed stunted and weak.

Now that his trial was over, Greg felt glad he had not chosen the easy path.

Facing forward, Greg sized up the landscape he had yet to traverse. Ahead was endless sidewalk – arrow straight and edged by parkland – stretching off into obscurity. To his right ran a line of swing sets, their seats swaying idly in the empty air… And there, just down the way, stood an ancient jungle gym – complete with disarranged wood chips – yet deserted of life. Beyond this random scattering of play equipment lurked…nothing – nothing at all—the ground conspicuously absent.

Alarm gripped him.

This highly dangerous location for a children's park – abutting an unguarded cliff - was ludicrous! Nevertheless, the sight of those creaking swings and worn slides, brought to mind fallen children, enticing him to stray from the path.

"You can't fool me that easy!" His voice was swallowed by the insubstantial air, sending chills down his spine. He shouldn't feel frightened -- not by a grassy park under a bright sun, right? Then again, was this place even real - or just some clever illusion hiding what was truly there?

Edging down the sidewalk, away from this eerie scene - his chills gradually subsided, driven away by the baking sun; its vigor promising to further intensify as the day wore on. He felt thankful for its presence guarding his back.

Ahead and to his right, just an arm's length off the path's edge, rested the aged gray surface of a shadow dappled picnic table, slumped against a gnarled oak. Greg paused to study the knife-scarred sagging boards with interest... For there, spread atop the initialed hearts of young lovers' short-lived infatuations, were the fixings of a birthday party. Something about the table, the cake, the whole idyllic scene, stirred a distant memory.

Without hesitating to consider, Greg stepped off the path to examine the bowed center of the dessert table. Suddenly, with a blur of motion the distant ledge rushed close, producing a sickening

vertigo! In an instant he was presented with an

impossible view—as he stared down on endless

emptiness! Stumbling back onto firm ground, Greg

gasped in relief as the treacherous cliff retreated,

returning to its previous limits. This place was

sadistic!

Cautiously, Greg edged a foot off the path. The

distant cliff—once again—proved to be an illusion,

for even as his big toe made contact with a knobby

root sticking up from the grass, the view reverted,

the aged tree also fading from existence. Greg's

foot rested only on stone. In truth, this table was

perched precariously atop the ledge.

He looked back at the table, examining the small

uneaten cake, all the while keeping a nervous eye on the devious cliff. In bright blue on white icing, the cake was inscribed "Happy Birthday, Greggory!" Unbidden, a memory surfaced of his mother, pastry bag in hand, skillfully applying the message to this cake…, a lifetime ago. Greg blinked in astonishment as one by one, six candles at the center of the cake ignited with tiny, unmoving flames.

Reaching out to check if any of this was real, his hand bumped a paper cup, nearly full to the brim with what could only be his mother's homemade lemonade. Another six cups clustered near his end of the table — all over-filled; something Greg well remembered his mother doing. Still half expecting some trick or illusion, Greg cautiously closed his

hand around the cup. As he carefully lifted the

wobbling liquid towards his mouth - something in

the reflection gave him pause.

It was not his hauntingly familiar features he

saw. Still, the young face he spied - swimming

among the ripples of his shaking hand - provoked

hazy memories.

The young child's nose and lips came close,

blotting out the reflection. In the next instant, the

level of liquid in the cup abruptly diminished.

Surprised, Greg dropped the cup. It thunked down,

perfectly upright on the table; not a single splash or

droplet escaping—the level of liquid still receding.

Glancing down at the array of cups, Greg

witnessed the reflection of his young self - some seven decades past - downing the last dregs of pulpy juice.

The reflections all shivered, their long ago surfaces rippling—as the boy's weight shifted the rickety table. In a haphazard fashion, the candles all puffed out — two momentarily missed — leaving not a trace of smoke pooling in the still air.

When the liquid finally settled, Greg's breath caught, his vision misting with tears. There stood his mother and father, looking so young and happy together, gazing down proudly at their son. Then a boyish exuberance had his young self urging his mother to cut the cake, and the past was once again awash in ripples.

Greg smiled as he raised a cup to his lips, watching the cake split into sections - the pieces - one by one - disappearing from the tray. How carefree his young life had been. He briefly considered taking a piece of cake before they were all gone - but didn't feel hungry.

At last, nodding sardonically to the capricious cliff, Greg stepped back onto the path - watching it nimbly retreat to lurk in the distance. He was startled to feel the cup vanish from his hand. Apparently, the rules of this place did not allow souvenirs.

Glancing up from his empty fingers, he blinked in surprise. The way ahead had changed. Now the sidewalk beneath him was altered, becoming the cracked asphalt of an old deserted school-ground.

CHAPTER 4

Greg mopped his brow—squinting into the distance. Ten minutes' brisk walk seemed to have gotten him nowhere—the scenery never varying, the distant cliff edge his constant companion. As far as the eye could see… lay an endless expanse of blacktop—badly repaired cracks running like tarred arteries across its surface; only a pair of faded white lines indicating where to walk. For long stretches these painted lines would fade altogether, forcing Greg to make certain he kept a straight line, never diverging. He wanted no repeat of what had occurred back at the picnic table.

The strips of tar were gummy in the sun, forcing Greg to step carefully. Despite the rocky surface's bumpiness, the thick calluses on his feet served him well, damping down the heat of the pavement.

Glancing up, Greg spotted a lone silhouette in the near distance. Hurrying forward, he saw to his relief a drinking fountain, located just off the path.

His throat parched, Greg stood facing the water basin sitting atop its base of cemented rock chips. He sized it up, trying to gauge if it was real. Reaching out a cautious hand, his fingers met hard stone.

When he stepped off the path, the distant cliff rushed close, the resulting vertigo turning his knees weak. Nevertheless he took the time to drink deeply from the jetting stream, not sure when he would get another chance. The arc of water - tinged pink in the sun's recalescent light – splattered noisily on the far edge of the tin catch basin… Yet it tasted amazing – sweet and pure.

With his thirst once more slaked, he turned to examine the reddish orb. Was it higher in the sky...or slightly lower? It seemed to him the rusty sun's lack of progression did not correlate to a slow sunrise, but a long sustained sunset. With this realization, Greg's internal compass rotated… Heading away from the sun - his assumed traveling direction was now west.

Beyond the fountain the way became rough, eroded chunks of paving hindering his progress. Looking up as he picked his way across an especially crumbled stretch, there -- close ahead -- the mist was back; chill and unwelcoming. Approaching steadily, it seemed more a solid wall than mere vapor.

As he pushed into the blinding grey, Greg kept his head low, barely able to make out his own feet; the sound of his muffled footsteps swallowed by the dense gloom. In mere seconds Greg was lost— the little sunlight managing to penetrate this blinding morass, seeming sickly and dull.

After a few more cautious steps, the mist rapidly
thinned, the subdued fore-drop of a parking lot
opening up before him; half the tar-graveled
spaces taken up by round-fendered cars. Here the
ground was wet from a recent rainstorm—a
multitude of dips in the pavement reflecting the
racing clouds like liquid mirrors.

A breeze picked up, shaping another fogbank
ahead. "What the..." Formed from a twisting white
swirl low to the ground, a small human shape rose
from the wall of grey. It formed into a young boy,
morosely hanging his head—coalescing features
cast in a grim light.

Terrified, Greg warily retreated, pressing up
against the wall of mist he'd just come through—

finding it to be damply solid! A vice of panic constricted Greg's chest. …But when the apparition made no move towards him — better yet, took no notice of him at all, he relaxed. Heart slowing, Greg began analyzing the situation. He recognized the era of clothing; "…and that hairstyle; late forties for sure".

Walking forward, the cloudy form fell to its knees before a particularly large puddle blocking the path, gazing down into its steely depths. Cautiously approaching its far side, Greg also peered in.

Reflected within its oil sheened murk, lay the weak shimmer of a sun fighting through obscuring clouds—ruling over a vivid scene from long ago.

Greg knelt carefully, his bare knees chill against the rough blacktop; shamed by what he saw.

The new kid, his hair carefully parted and slicked back, looked around at a gang of schoolyard bullies, trying not to flinch at their aggressive taunts. He clutched at his books, edging towards a gap in their huddle, until one of the larger boys pushed him back into the circle. The guy's sneering mouth moved to form the words "Where d'yuh think your goin?"

Next, a smaller boy stepped forward from the encircling group. Hesitating for an instant, he tore the books from the kid's arms, scattering them into the puddle; washing away the memory in a cascade of ripples…

(Greg jerked his head back, water splattering his face. Hurriedly wiping his eyes, Greg found he had a mental image which continued the events.)

…His initiation complete, young Greg turned and stalked away, already ashamed of what he had done. The other three bullies quickly finished the job; knocking the kid over and drenching his jeans.

Now, as the surface calmed, Greg angled his head, watching through the shivering water as they followed after his young self, slapping him on the back.

Looking up from this reflected memory; at the

child made of shifting fog, Greg frowned, perplexed. "Why are you here?" There was no response from the illusion; no indication it had heard. Not liking his options, but seeing no alternative, Greg stepped around the now blank puddle. Drawing as close as he dared to the grey form, he tried edging around it. His foot met treacherous emptiness! Wind-milling his arms, Greg prevented himself from falling over the cliff, only by throwing himself sideways; thus making contact with the shrouded form.

As Greg suspected, the boy was no more than vapor—dissolving instantly. Still, a coldness seeped into his being, as if his soul had been doused. His mind was beset by this child's emotions.

Battered by the boy's impotent rage, Greg scrambled to his feet and ran, thinking to break free of this intense suffering.

He stumbled on through the fog, each puddle he splashed through driving needles of cold into his bare feet. Finally, unable to tell in which direction the cliff might lie, Greg forced himself to slow; the thought of falling into its abyss, terrifying him far more than the alien presence blanketing his mind. He clutched at his head, fighting the insinuating emotions.

Labored breathing sounding loud in his ears, Greg inched forward, dreading the cliff edge. With each foot gained, the mental pain sharpened. His legs were growing stiff, as if each step required them to be pulled through cold molasses. The fog about him thickened, growing water logged. It seemed to be putting up a resistance all its own. He would eventually be forced to stop, or risk suffocation!

The ground began to tilt; gravity slowly shifting from under him, forcing him to lean over to keep from toppling. The cliff was reaching out to claim him!

There seemed to be only one way out. Letting down his mental barrier, the influx of emotions entered his mind. They were intensely pervasive; forcing him to review the scene from the boy's perspective.

The kid was new in town, wanting desperately

to fit in. So had Greg; which was why he had shifted the bullies' attention to the new kid.

Gritting his teeth, Greg clutched his head, fighting to remember his long ago justification, though it felt so inadequate. "I only scattered those books to make the other boys quit bullying me—to pick on someone else for a change. I never harmed anyone!"

One by one, Greg's justifications were stripped from him, as the repercussions of his actions invaded his comprehension. The child's parents were forced to buy their son new books; books they could ill afford. It became much harder for the boy to find friends, spending weeks alone at school, isolated; his primary interaction with those around him, taunts as the kid who wet his pants.

Greg was forced to his knees by the cliff's reaching grasp, the mental turmoil compelling him to accept that it was he whom the kid had despised that day.

Grimacing, Greg dropped to his belly, gripping the rocky bitumen to keep from sliding.

"I'm so sorry!" he yelled into the swirling maelstrom. He expected the apology to make little difference, yet it did. The heavy turmoil of his thoughts transforming the air about him, abruptly ceased. The mist began to thin – gravity's pendulum reorienting beneath him. Greg knew it was not the apology that had saved him, but the acknowledgement of his culpability. He rose shakily

to his feet, pain ebbing from his battered chest.

CHAPTER 5

As the fog cleared, Greg found himself standing upon evenly mown grass, striated by white lines every five yards. Looking behind… the perfect grass stretched on far as the eye could see.

Ahead, Greg spotted a familiar orange water cooler. Like the sporadic water breaks given during high school football practice, he trotted forward expectantly—his thirst poignant, despite his recent saturation from the mist. Approaching the long aluminum bench upon which it sat, he crouched in the turf, lifting the half full cooler from the metal seat.

The distant cliff rushed in close! Now the bench was mounted directly to the cliff edge. Defiant, Greg ignored it.

Balancing the sloshing jug overhead, he drained the ice cold water into his mouth, remembering what his mean-tempered high school coach had always yelled when he caught his players doing this. "Hey moron, that's what cups are for!"

Fingers slipping on its perspiring base - Greg clutched at the jug to prevent it from crashing down. His hand caught on something mounted to the side, tearing it free. Gripped in Greg's hand was the smooth cylinder of a well-stocked cup dispenser. Looking at it with chagrin, he now knew why his coach had forbidden the practice.

Though elongated and distorted by the plastic tube, this was Greg's first real chance to examine his reflection… He was darn handsome -- his nose more refined, cheekbones prominent -- with deep set eyes a brilliant blue.

Their vibrancy dimmed, a sudden waning of light darkening his features with a pall of fear. For there… off to his left came a swirling of cloud, reflected along the side of the plastic cylinder—the onward stretching field metamorphosing into a dark abstract of his baser deeds.

Dreading the sight, Greg raised his eyes from his distorted reflection. The way ahead had indeed become ominous, roiling with angry cauldrons of whirling mist. "I barely made it past grade school…

how can I face my betrayal?!" Squaring his

shoulders, Greg stepped into the enveloping fog.

Pressing blindly forward, Greg's worst fears

were confirmed, as the initial curtain of cold vapor

was swept aside; for there, in the eye of this

maelstrom of mist, a human form uncoiled.

Backpedaling, he cried out in despair; "I can't,

not her!" It was the hairstyle of the evolving figure

he recognized first, as she knelt weightless on the

grass, head bowed.

Greg burst through the wall of mist - trailers of

cloud briefly clinging to him like a defensive tackle—sprinting down the grassy field in a parody of his glory days. Light seemed to warp before his eyes, the distance dilating, until ahead lay the familiar signpost, and beyond it the cave entrance. "Where has everything gone?!"

Glancing back, he saw the fog was still pursuing him! He ran all the faster—for just visible within its ominous depths, came the slow walking figure of shrouded grey. Dashing straight for the dark maw from which this nightmare journey had begun - he felt a rubbery snap as if a dozen bungee cords had broken, as he swept past the ward that had previously denied him entry.

Greg sat up with an excruciating jerk, his body

horribly stiff. A white sheet previously draped over him came sliding off. His wide staring eyes lacked proper focus, making an indistinct blur of the startled man in a doctor's coat; scalpel in hand, gesturing urgently at him. The tall man's deep voice boomed loud in his ears. "No, you must go back!" Greg couldn't move so much as a finger; yet his dying nervous system had him silently screaming in agony, his every nerve on fire! The tunnel tugged insistently, and having no ability to prevent it, he slipped away.

An irresistible yank pulled him back through the cave mouth, to land sprawling on the same mountainous trailhead. Miraculously unhurt, he scrambled to his feet, quaking at the memory of his dead flesh. The revulsion of it made him turn away from the cave mouth—and there, just beyond the path marker, roiled the cloud of life's accusations. As the fog enveloped the sign post, Greg found himself trapped, pressed against the invisible barrier to the real world—his last chance to avoid this confrontation to slip past the blockade and escape along the downward sloping path. But he did not retreat. He could no longer run from her.

Addressing the figure of mist… "I miss you, Sage." …he stepped into her embrace.

Wrapping his arms around her insubstantial form, she dissolved reluctantly. For an instant he perceived the feel of her, wetly clinging to his bare skin -- bringing with it a sense of loss. The ache in his chest seemed far too physical to be mere emotion.

The vision of that day, the day he had always looked back on with regret, confronted him. His high school girlfriend was seated on the ground, knees drawn up under her skirt, head in her hands. As young Greg had turned to leave, she looked up at him with red rimmed eyes, reaching out a beseeching hand. Greg remembered how badly he had wanted to comfort her. Instead, he had hurriedly walked away.

His justifications were pitiful. Sage had been rather short and bookish; definitely not the cheerleader type. She had been poor, and he had needed real money to make his computer hardware ideas a reality. Dating the richest girl in school had only added to Sage's grief; grief Greg was now forced to feel. "How long had her heartbreak lasted?" He wished he could crawl away from this torture. His one remaining option, to drop off the cliff to oblivion, was something he could not bring himself to do; so he stayed there, unmoving, barely feeling the cold gravel biting into his knees, taking the emotional lashing he had so long deserved.

Knowing how badly this decision had altered her life, tears came to his eyes. "Forgive me... forgive me Sage." He knew no mere words would ever be enough to make up for his rejection, but within moments the mist was gone.

With a heavy heart he stood, brushing off his

knees. Glancing at the sign to make sure of his way,

he resumed life's journey.

CHAPTER 6

Between one step and the next, the scene abruptly changed; the rubble-strewn mountain ascent transforming into even linoleum beneath his feet. Walls solidified to both sides, completing the illusion of an office corridor from his computer programming days; exact, down to the inept still life painting of anemic fruit on the wall.

Greg now understood what was occurring. These memories of his life were not actual places; more like overlays to the 'true path'.

This corridor however, retained this portion of

the trail's upward slant. It made for slippery going on the recently mopped linoleum.

Surely this place was mocking him, for there to his right stood a yellow 'Caution, floor is wet!' sign. The picture was not the standard one of a cartoon man with no feet slipping over backward, but that of a real man, Greg no doubt, tumbling over a cliff edge with arms flailing.

The macabre sign was the last straw. If this place was trying to frighten him, it failed. All he felt was anger. Walking past the sign, he kicked it. Skittering across the floor and turning to mist, it fell right through the wall.

Ahead, the quality of the wallpaper grew more expensive, even as his bolstering career had become more successful. He gratefully stopped at an ugly water cooler he had drunk from many a time, as a lowly IT worker. As he stepped nearer the gurgling blue canister, the walls folded back and away to reveal the truth. He was on a rising ramp of stone, growing ever narrower. Glancing up along the path, he saw that the way ahead would become truly perilous.

Greg retreated from the cliff - the plasticky taste of the water still fresh in his mouth — watching the overlay of a marble corridor take hold, marking the ascent.

This hall of business he had once so proudly strode in clicking dress shoes – (the swish of his silken slacks, and the tight folds of his custom tailored dress shirt rolled halfway up his strong forearms, making him feel stylishly debonair) - now felt hollow and empty of importance. The fact that it led to the literal overview of his company, on the top floor of his 50 story PC marketing firm, had only served to further bolster his ego.

The hall stretched on much longer than it had in life, the ascent physically wearing. Reaching a polished brass fountain, he halted in relief. As he stepped from the center of the hall, the walls and floor abruptly vanished, revealing dual precipices, startlingly close! In reality, he stood on a narrow ridgeline between two peaks—and just feet to either side; a devastating drop to infinity! The fountain was real—perched precariously atop a thin outcropping. No way was he going to risk his afterlife, for just a drink of water.

Greg stepped away from the brass fountain - (the hall reforming around him) - and plodded tiredly on, determinedly making his way up the center of the wide hall. He was feeling more and more exhausted with each step; an ache now forming in his lower back. A minute passed; two minutes. His body felt on the verge of collapse.

Stopping to rest, he glanced up and groaned. Just ahead was the same brass fountain, set back against the illusive marble wall. He should have known something like this would happen. The need

for a drink, no matter how foolhardy, had become

a prerequisite; for it seemed without it, he might

spend forever plodding along this particular stretch

of life.

Cautiously, he made his way out onto the stone

outcrop; every step a careful test. The cracks

beneath his feet shifted ominously, grinding, even

buckling in places; yet somehow the stone held,

allowing him to reach the fountain. Pushing the

lever, he took a small sip of water. It was bitter and

metallic tasting, but immediately helped quench

his thirst.

Not daring to wait any longer - he turned and

leapt for the path. With a loud crack and rumble,

the fountain shifted, tipping outwards and down

even as he turned back to watch; stones breaking

loose and raining into the abyss. Then the marble

hall faded back into sight, showing only a slight

discoloration on the wall where the fountain had

been. Breathing a huge sigh of relief, Greg turned

to study the sloping ramp of worldly gain. As

expected, the way ahead had turned moist and

gloomy.

A motion caught his eye. Across the reflective

floor strode a pair of feminine legs, igniting that old

familiar thrill_towards a woman who - even while

shamelessly flaunting herself - had organized

Greg's finances back in the heyday of his business

empire. But she had left the moment things had

gotten tough! Greg had to admit her seduction had been at least partially successful, signaling the death knell to his already failing marriage.

He watched her reflection pass - a growing ache of shame in his throat and chest - recalling his fantasies.

Her 'sophisticated' reflection was swallowed by a swamp of mist.

"So… where are the hidden dry ice machines?" His nervous chuckle edged on hysteria, at the thought of confronting yet another weakness.

Walking through the mist, his bare feet slipped on the smooth floor; slick with trickles of water.

Going down on all fours, he scrambled through the dense filter of brume; the scene at last opening up before him.

Linda sat pertly in her cloudy desk chair, busy typing legal documents; just one of her multifaceted array of skills. Her body of shapely grey mist wore nothing but her underclothing! Remembering how often he had undressed her with his eyes, he realized this was how he had truly seen her; not as an equal, nor even his employee, but only as a woman he desired. He glanced away, feeling appalled with himself.

Impatiently scrambling across the slippery floor, he bulldozed through the mirage. He needn't have bothered. Her form had no real substance; dispersing into tattered coils. Greg breathed a sigh of relief.

A wall of mist came crashing down, a wave of forlorn resignation sending him sliding backwards along the hall, choking on the spumes of mist_threatening to drown him! Gasping for breath, he was forced to view events from her perspective.

Greg had hired Linda right out of college; a decade of student loans riding on her success as his personal assistant. Now that he had her view on events - could feel each of her worries – (the knot in her stomach every time she checked the mailbox, sure to find yet another bill she couldn't pay) - it was only a matter of time before she became desperate enough to use her body for advancement. Nevertheless, it had been his lonely gaze on her - his own marriage on the edge of failure for years - that had led her to this conclusion.

But why did she have to wear those provocatively short skirts? …Because he had, whether intentionally or not, led her on.

"I never actually did anything!" That had always been Greg's justification. He was now learning, thought begets action.

…Deceiving herself; telling herself she just wanted what was best for her children, Linda had started her 'campaign' at the office. Worse still, she had a loving husband; "but surely what he doesn't know, won't hurt him," she had thought. "I am... only doing this for my family."

As the weeks passed and her boss never put his thoughts into action, she had inevitably become guilty. Her husband had felt her emotional withdrawal, and threatened to file for divorce. Only through quitting her job had she saved their marriage.

His perception altering, Greg now saw her letter of resignation in a new light; no longer thinking of her as inconsiderate, but driven to it by his own weakness.

He had been planning to promote her to vice president. If only he had made the workplace strictly professional, there would have been no reason to leave. Their family lives, his fortune, even his employees... All had suffered from his own 'personal' fantasies.

This was a new concept for Greg. Before this revelation, he had always imagined his 'inner' thoughts as harmless; conveniently overlooking all the times when the opposite had been true.

CHAPTER 7

Greg trudged on in tired resignation… each
footstep resounding wetly along a plaster hall;
occasional alcoves marking the inset doors of
courtrooms …another cloud billowing before him.

Glancing up - expecting to find the manikin
shadow of his divorced wife - he felt a jolt of
apprehension, for interspersed within the fogbank
arose a multitude of shapes.

"It looks like your GRU (guilt rendering unit)
could benefit from an upgrade in high performance
RAM. I have connections... I'm sure I could

negotiate a bulk discount deal." Speaking to the

mist, Greg was unsure who he was addressing;

God? Levity and bantering was Greg's way of

dealing with stressful situations, but it was no joke

how many people he now faced.

Their office garb left him wondering, "were

these my company's employees?"

Walking into the crowds of people, he hunched

his shoulders against the bitter barrage of

emotions… Here a woman unable to pay rent;

there a man feeling inadequate with the loss of his

job, and unable to provide for his family.

Individually, their anger towards him was

bearable - only a small hindrance - but as he

pressed on, he staggered under the weight of

countless mental whispers. The sheer number of them jumbled his thoughts, a thousand emotions and voices all clamoring for his attention. He was mentally drowning, unable to distinguish his own consciousness from the morass of desperate and dejected humanity!

Using a mental trick he had learned in programming - when his brain had become scrambled by an endless line of code - he concentrated on a single thought, "How could I have wronged all these people?"

The multitude of distraught voices would not be suppressed - returning to the forefront of his mind and sweeping aside any clarity of thought -- as they jostled against each other to express their grievances. Changing tack, he tried listening carefully to first one, then another of these people's woes, but every time_the individual's testimony was swallowed by the clamor.

The shock of his knees hitting the floor… the fact that he was clutching his head, thumbs massaging his temples -- barely registered. Fear blossomed in the tumult; his panic or theirs', he could not distinguish. He was deafened by the thunder of sensations, his individuality slipping away. He was drowning in the cacophony!

Repeating his name in a frantic mantra, "…Greggory Mason, Greggory Mason, Greg...," he struggled to find clarity; not to discern his offenses, but simply to beg for silence. "Please, I need help" he cried out, unsure if it was his voice speaking aloud, or the others demanding compensation, their cries growing persistently louder.

"I can't do this alone! Pleeease!" With a dull flare of pain his forehead struck the floor. But no, it was not hard stone; rather pebbled earth against his brow.

A light blossomed from within, a wave of compassion sweeping over him; not obliterating the voices, instead restoring their individuality— giving Greg freedom to think, ponder, and remember. The answer came.

Busy with his divorce proceedings – (trying to stay ahead of his wife's underhanded lawyers) -- when his company stockholders had agreed to buy out a smaller, failed PC brand, he had left negotiations to his legal team, not reading the fine print. His lack of oversight had led to a company downsizing in the merger.

In the final settlement of their divorce, 'Irene the Terrible' had tried to take everything from him. He had lost most of his wealth; but his true wealth, his children, were the real reason he had devoted all his time to the divorce trial. Had that been the right thing to do? "Surely!"

But… if he had taken just a little more time …came the adamant thought - he could have saved many of their jobs. Instead he had fixated entirely upon his own family's needs.

He wanted to deny his guilt—surely he was

more responsible for his children than to these strangers!

This was undoubtedly true, but by building a business empire as he had, he took at least partial responsibility for the welfare of his entire workforce. With this realization, one by one the voices were appeased and dispersed—his thoughts again his own.

Still, guilt weighed heavily upon his shoulders… "How many peoples' lives have I ruined?!" …trying to understand why, after all he had done, he was being allowed to continue—why he had been exonerated.

His unworthiness urged him to surrender; leap off that hungry cliff. Still, some part of him was not convinced of his ignobility. Climbing to his feet, he

stepped forward; once again feeling the warmth of

the sun.

CHAPTER 8

Squinting, Greg's eyes were dazzled by the fiery

sun's reflected glare off white concrete. Rubbing

his aching forehead (hand shading his eyes), he

automatically turned up the familiar front walk

leading to the upscale suburban home of his

middle years... And froze in horror; expecting at

any moment the ground to collapse beneath him!

Yet the scene held.

Cautiously stepping onto the stoop, he peered in

the front entry of a house awash in memories—

recollections of a single father in his late forties

struggling to raise his two youngest, swimming into focus on the glass:

Consoling Brett that the bullies at his new school were in fact the weak ones…

…Waiting up late for his children on a Friday night…

…Hugging a heartbroken Karen on the top step, wishing he could shield her from the pain.

Reaching out to touch Karen's tearstained face, pressed against her father's shoulder, Greg's hand made no impact on the reflected scene. Nor did the image dissolve as his hand passed through. Something here had changed. The illusions were more solid, almost tangible to his touch.

Yet like all Greg's past haunts, this scene was but

a figment of mortality; yielding not a sight nor sound of occupancy. The hum of lawnmowers, the barking of territorial dogs, the happy giggles and shouts of children at play; all were distinctly absent. Here, there was utter silence; devoid of his more unpleasant memories:

…Forbidding Karen from attending her senior prom, only to find that offending cigarette had belonged to a friend she was protecting from a third strike…

…His uneasy resignation when Brett joined 'that superstitious cult of hypocrites'…

…Not even the unfortunate downsizing of his company that had lost still more of his employees their jobs — an avoidable loss; if he hadn't spent most of his time working from home, caring for his children.

Returning to the path, careful to place the vehement red orb at his back, he set out, thankful his deeply tanned skin kept him from burning. His thirst was another matter—every breath rasping against a parched throat.

The first evidence of water came long before he spotted the gushing garden hose, far down the way - seemingly abandoned by a careless homeowner a few feet from the sidewalk - causing a multitude of wet ribbons to stain across the tilted cement. The flood ran over the rounded curb, streaming along the gutter until reaching a storm drain, some two blocks away.

Getting down on his hands and knees, Greg reached for the hose, his balance shifting precariously.

"Come on, just a few more inches!" He strained a little further and... With a desperate cry, he fell forward, his supporting hand slipping on the wet concrete.

Certain of his doom, he twisted sideways, windmilling his arms to make a last desperate grab for the sidewalk.

With a splat, his shoulder and face hit the sodden grass. Greg was so surprised to find the lawn was real - each of the stiff and living bristles cool and springy beneath his cheek - that he found himself shaking -- but whether in laughter or tears he could not tell; likely both.

Fearful of the cliff`s sudden return, Greg snatched up the hose and leapt onto the sidewalk. Between shaky breaths, he filled his mouth with water, the excess splattering against his feet, pleasantly cool.

The water tasted incredible; like a mountain spring at its source—but alive with something more! Lifting the hose over his head, he let sparkling water cascade over his body; dousing his fear and sweeping away the weight of guilt -- leaving him strong and refreshed.

Though physically rejuvenating, the cleansing went far deeper—removing the crushing weight of shame that had clung to him ever since beginning this journey—finally recognizing its presence in his previous life; his every selfish act compounding the burden.

A wave of gratitude at his reprieve sent him to his knees.

Greg sobbed brokenly; his throat constricting with emotion.

The intensity of this experience left his body aching, yet it was an exquisite pain he wanted to endure. He felt the presence of the one who had taken upon Himself the burden of Greg's sin; a deity Greg was humbled to realize, had been with him on his journey every step of the way.

It was a father's love, reminding Greg of when, as a little boy curled in his parent's bed; he had felt safe and enfolded in their tender protection. At long last Greg understood what his son Brett had meant about becoming renewed.

Gradually the manifestation of compassionate strength ebbed and faded. Still, it lingered on in his memory, illuminating all the self-centered ambitions Greg's soul had long harbored — not blotting out Greg's mistakes, but shielding him from their affects; reminding him there was hope for something better.

At last, wiping his eyes, Greg stood tall, freed from the penalties of his own injustices. The way had been paved, but his journey was not yet over.

Examining the hose, Greg recognized the faded pink stripe running its length. Glancing up at the yellow residence - with its flower-lined wraparound porch and upper veranda - he grinned, then laughed in open delight. It was Mrs. Jensen's house; the very woman - so long ago - who had invited Brett to her youth group. The woman was long gone, but it seemed the effects of her friendly invitation to join them had lingered, waiting for a time when Greg was ready.

Setting the hose back on the grass — where it could continue nourishing her lawn — Greg turned to continue his journey… and froze. Half a block ahead drifted a white mist, radiant with infused sunlight.

Given plenty of time to ponder what new apparitions might appear, Greg trod readily forward along the hot sidewalk, stepping at last into the waiting truth.

One moment, he was in a high end suburban neighborhood, and the next, he was encapsulated by glowing mist; feeling welcomed rather than condemned.

Here there was no confrontation. Nevertheless, ahead stood two forms; tall and confident, though not yet fully grown – his two youngest children as they were in high school – facing away from him, towards whatever lay ahead. Stepping between them, he placed a hand on their shoulders. Their presence entered his mind even as their manifestations faded, speaking to him in the form of memories and emotions, rather than words.

Sorting through his life, they addressed the many 'mistakes' he had made as a single father, but rather than forming a negative opinion, his two youngest thought of those tough times as inconsequential—humorous anecdotes of an otherwise happy home. He had shown his love not only by the physical security he had given them, but through the time he had spent with them; demonstrating with action his affection and pride.

Those employees who had lost their jobs to further downsizing, had not actually blamed him personally. Many of them had families of their own, and had understood his need to be there for

his. In a moment of inspiration Greg˙s entire

outlook on life changed, finally realizing it was not

what he had done - or let happen - that had

influenced people˙s respect for him, but their

discernment of his intentions.

CHAPTER 9

Greg curled blistered toes in the cool beach sand near his small retirement home on a peaceful north pacific shore—listening to the crashing of breakers in the middle distance; familiarly soothing.

Leaning out from the rutted trail to grab the water bottle perched conveniently atop his weathered gate post, he took a long draw. Surveying his cozy haven, the urge was strong to swing open the squeaky gate and check over his ripening garden, dominated by the red of tomatoes, bell peppers and strawberries. Instead,

with a last look at his small seaside home, he

turned away - water bottle in hand - ready to

traverse the final stretch of his life.

It no longer seemed to matter if he kept to the

path. When he strayed, the abyss did not appear;

failing to spring into existence as it had so many

times before. Yet he remained close to the trail,

not wanting to tempt fate after having come so far.

Ahead marched many a long row of glistening

dunes, their coarse white sand sparkling in the

evening light—only occasionally broken here and

there by tall mounds of brownish dune grass.

"These are more like hills than dunes" he

grumbled - trudging up one side and skittering

down the far slope of a particularly grueling hillock.

At this rate, he would be spending as much time

going up and down as making forward progress. It

made him long for the flatter, grittier dunes closer

to shore.

Instead he stuck to this never-meandering path.

It hadn't led him astray yet. And the way was

manageable; for the living water had alleviated not

only the anguish of his battered conscience, but

the discomfort of his battered feet as well.

Slowly the shoreline came curving in towards his

path. By the time he had navigated another dozen

dunes, he was looking down on the tideline.

A frigid sea breeze made him shiver. This place felt like many a late autumn day when he had walked this beach in an aging body - wearing a warm turtleneck to resist the chill; as he had pondered the accomplishments and failures of his life.

Cresting a rise, he saw at a particularly low point between the next two dunes, a shallow tide pool. Running down the steep slope, he looked into the glittering reflection; hoping for that certain memory. Serendipitously, the breeze tossed ripples died down, the surface slowly stilling. And there, reflected in the water, came two figures walking hand in hand.

Headed towards the pool was an old man Greg scarcely recognized as himself, and at his side, an elderly woman.

As the two slightly stooped figures ambled closer, he strained to hear her voice, yet the reflection remained but a silent mimicry.

Reading her lips, Greg watched the scene unfold, this time as an outside observer. "Why do you still hold on to so much of your wealth? Has it bought you happiness? Susan tells me all you do these days is wander the seashore."

Both old and young Greg knelt stiffly in the reflection of sand, waves, and reddening sky. "I have many regrets." He quoted his own lines from that final year of his life, even as the wrinkled lips moved silently. "The one thing that could make me happy, is taking back the words I once said to you, long ago."

The man in the reflection reached up, taking the small, liver spotted hand of the woman standing before him; declaring: I don't deserve you; not after what I did; but I have to ask you anyway; Sage, will you marry me?" The grey-haired woman nodded her head emphatically, tears of happiness falling from her eyes, yet there was a tinge of sadness in her smile. Grabbing both his proffered hands, she pulled him to his feet with surprising vigor—yet continued staring down at her own feet, her words a whisper. "Greg, the doctors have given me only two months to live."

The young of body, yet world-weary man,

turned away from the tear spattered reflection.

The breeze blown ripples instantly returned,

playing across its briny surface, dissolving the

reflection of the redeemed couple heading back

towards a golden sun, arms tight around each

other. Now the tidal inlet was empty; only deep

footprints troubled the sand.

That single season they had been given, had

been the happiest, and saddest possible ending to

a long life — Sage had died peacefully in her sleep.

That same day, Greg had departed with her in

mind, if not spirit.

Her last words he would always remember, the night before he would waken to find her cold body next to his. "I'm fading Greggory. I find myself slipping about in this body, as though my soul no longer fits." He had leaned in to kiss her cheek but she had pushed him back, with a strength that still bellied her fragile appearance.

"Back in high school, people wondered why I gave Greggory Mason a second glance. It's what you had in here..." She tapped him on his chest. "Owhh careful, my heart isn't what it used to be." Her shoulders shook briefly in silent mirth, but her expression remained serious. "...And not because of what is in here." Her steady finger had tapped him on the forehead, much to his bemusement.

"I'll be waiting for you on the other side," she had said, laying her small head on his chest. The feeling of rightness - her head and arm against his tired old body - had made Greg forget what he was going to ask her on that final night they had together; "The other side of what?" Now he knew.

Young Greg remembered every moment she had graced him with, and wondered why she had not been waiting by the pool. The immanent sunset instilled in him a sense of dire urgency. His time was running out. For the setting sun had altered, looking unusually weak and burgundy hued—his elongated shadow before him on the path, tinging to the appearance of stilled blood.

He thought of the shiny scalpel the shocked mortician had been brandishing; when his body had sat up abruptly beneath the white sheet. How her shoulders would shake in laughter at the morbidity of that story.

His discolored shadow grew shorter as he approached a particularly steep dune, and with difficulty, began climbing up the loose sand on tired legs. At last cresting the rise, he was disheartened to discover this was only a miniature foothill compared to the much mightier summit looming ahead; the sand on it much coarser, more like small mountain-pebbles.

He glanced back the way he had come. Gone was his passage through mortality; for, far below -

just a mile or so back along a boulder strewn path - was the dark cave mouth.

Had he passed some test then; proven the value of his existence?

Now that he was past the illusions of his former life, he could look down and see each section of his journey; from the flat stretch just after the initial boulder riddled ascent, where he had been presented with his youthful failures; to the thin ridgeline where he had ascended the nerve-racking years to his career's pinnacle; and finally the half mile stretch of broad path leading up to this hill on which he now stood, filled with wavy undulations near the end to represent the many sand dunes he had scaled. His journey was almost over. He could feel it.

Turning back to face the way not yet traveled, his weary eyes widened in disbelief. Above him towered a steep conical mountain of jagged grey stone, bathed in reddish light. Easily a hundred feet up - near the pinnacle of bare rock - could be seen a second cave, glowing faintly with reflected light.

CHAPTER 10

His goal at long last in sight, Greg half climbed, half crawled up the rocky slope, grabbing at boulders and bunches of sparse grass to keep from sliding back down the stony path.

He toiled on, taking frequent sips from his water bottle. Finally, feeling for another handhold, Greg's palm came to rest on the sheer rock face, marking the last leg of his ascent. He glanced up with an exhausted sigh. Above him towered the rugged rock face; the only way forward a series of inset handholds going straight up a perfectly smooth strip of vertical cliff.

Easing onto a boulder pressed against the foot of the cliff, he slumped back against the rough stone, looking out on a hazy view. In the far distance, the sun was dipping towards an indistinct, flat black line of horizon, its bottom curve nearly touching the edge of this world.

Pulling the bottle from his waistband, he drained the last few mouthfuls; then, letting the empty container slip from his hand, he watched it roll and bounce down the long slope. Soon it was lost from sight among the shattered boulders, their mineral rich layers reflecting the sun's last dying glare.

His rest was cut short, for as the massively swollen sun touched the horizon, it bowed oddly, turning a sickly purple along its bottom edge.

Quakes rippled through the ground; at first sensed

only as a growing vibration in his bones. In an

instant though, a rumbling began; the scanty

covering of pebbles beneath his feet, juddering and

sliding away.

Whirling around he clutched at the cliff face,

relieved to find easy purchase on the evenly spaced

and well-formed hand holds. Unlike the shifting

rock beneath his feet, the cliff held steady. No

telling how long that would last though. Time to

get going!

The climb was easy; his hands sure in their placement, the path straight and true up the rock surface.

Glancing down, Greg's stomach lurched. The trail he had ascended, the entire mountainous expanse, was gone; the world was gone! Beneath him stretched an endless black—'THE VOID' had returned, and was quickly laying claim to this world.

Forcing himself to look away from the terrifying sight, he groaned; for immediately above him swirled a wall of grey. Resignedly, he climbed upward and was engulfed by cloud.

A few steps up into the blinding mist - his hands and feet fumbling for the next holds - he emerged into the cloud's hollow center. Seeing the familial

shape that stood above him on the cliff face, he let

out a joyful cry; delighted to see his granddaughter.

"Suzie!"

Glancing down at him in surprise, her hand flew

to her chest in shock, her eyebrows lowering in

confusion. She was so lifelike; surely not just an

illusion. She spoke slowly, her voice uncertain.

"Grandfather, is that you?" Her full lips pursed in

concern, taking in his battered and exhausted

state.

Greg clung to the rock, speechless, his head

tilted back to face his grandchild. She was dressed

in pajamas, her eyes heavy and swollen; yet she

was still lovely, her face suffused with equal parts

wonder and sadness. "Grandpa, I miss you so much!"

He had to stop himself from climbing up the last few grips to try and physically comfort her. "I know Suzie, but don't worry. I'm on my way to a happier place… I'm sure of it."

"At the hospital…" Suzie trailed off, her shoulders beginning to shake.

He smiled comfortingly. "There at the end, I felt your hand. I worried I would never have the chance to say goodbye."

Crouching down so they were on the same level, she reached out a hand towards him.

"Wait Suzie, don't touch me. You'll…disappear." Tears came to Susan's eyes, but she hurriedly wiped them away, looking around

uncertainly. "What is this place? Why do you look

so... different?"

Feeling the cliff give a brief shudder, Greg

interrupted her questions, speaking quickly.

"Susan, I don't have much time, so I need you to

think carefully. Is there...any way that I've wronged

you?!"

Seeing the look of confusion on her face, and

feeling the cliff shift yet again, - (the rumbles were

becoming more persistent) - his voice grew

desperate. "Please Susan, think!"

Susan's countenance turned bleak, tears

dripping from her eyes—falling onto his upturned

face; dissolving into puffs of mist. At the same time

droplets of moisture began beading against the cliff, trickling down the stone as if it too were crying; forming into rivulets that ran into the holds to which he clung.

He didn't dare shift his grip on the slick stone. He could see the horrible possibility in his mind's eye; his hands losing their grip--before falling away to his doom, only Susan to witness him tumbling out of sight through the cloud; never knowing for certain_what had become of him.

"What is it Suzie? What have I done? I've given everything to you; my fortune, my love, all that I possess!"

Susan shook her head sadly, more tears dripping from her golden lashes. "Grandpa, if you had only agreed to move in with us, you could have made it to the hospital in plenty of time!"

"I didn't…want to be a burden to you."

Susan smiled sadly. "No grandpa, it was your pride that kept you away." Her voice turned wistful. "If you had stayed with us, you could have taught me so much. As it is, I don't know how to manage your finances."

Greg's arms shook, his fingers beginning to ache. "You're right. I'm sorry. I should have been there… I should have prepared you."

"But why give all your stocks to me? Uncle John has lost his business. He's filing for bankruptcy! He can no longer support his family!"

"Why doesn't he go suck up to his mother like

he always does," was Greg's immediate thought. Out loud he gasped "I gave you everything because I know you'll use my money responsibly."

Susan's hands clenched into fists. "Your son is in poverty!"

At her words, something tightened in Greg's gut, even as a hardened inner part of him softened. He finally realized who else had thought like this. 'Irene the Terrible'; she who had once tried to take everything from him. In his own way, he was acting every bit as despicable.

"You're right, Suzie! Help my eldest son. Please, give him what he needs to get back on his feet."

Her form little more than a blur for the tears in his eyes, Susan leaned toward him. The instant her lips touched his forehead, in a final goodbye, she —

and the cloud about her, began fading away, her

voice growing ever more distant. "I love you,

Grandf..." She was gone.

A shifting from below made Greg instinctively

leap upwards, just as his foothold broke away. An

instant later the whole mountain let out a great

lurching rumble. Clinging desperately to the higher,

dry stone, Greg looked down to see the cliff below

him inexorably crumbling; great chunks of stone

falling into the abyss.

The shuddering at last subsided, and he began

to climb at a near run, dashing vertically towards

the summit; still some 50 feet distant. Several

times he barely managed to keep ahead of the

dissolving cliff; chunks of weakened stone breaking loose all around him.

The bloody sun no longer warmed his straining back - its bottom curve sunk beneath the fathomless horizon - being consumed by an impenetrable black veil—an emptiness far deeper than a mere absence of light.

This body, while young and agile, ached from the day's long travel—swiftly draining the last of his energy. He was pushing past the edge of his physical endurance—still a dozen feet from attaining the summit — his movements becoming sluggish, as the stone beneath him weakened. Gravity was steadily intensifying; the vacuous entity dragging at his soles—as if wishing to claim his very soul.

Another quake brought him up short -- tortured wrists and arms aching_as he clung desperately to the stone. Precious seconds slipped by as he waited out the quake, giving him little chance to rest.

The entire cliff quavered, accompanied by a splintering sound overhead. Glancing up, eyes widening in horror, he witnessed a black line snaking horizontally across the cliff face, growing into a jagged split, threatening at any moment to separate this cliff from the peak.

Terrified, he watched as a car sized chunk of stone broke free from under the peak, ricocheting off the widening fault with a loud shattering crack—sending it down in a twisting spin. Judging its trajectory, Greg swung far out to the side; callused fingers straining to keep their grip on the textured stone. A blast of air buffeted him, the elongated stone twisting around him as it fell past, with only inches to spare! Swinging back the other way, Greg's feet had barely found purchase on the bruising stone, before he was again climbing.

Only a few feet from his goal, he made a desperate leap, springing up and away from the widening rift. Time slowed to a crawl, while beneath him the wall of stone dropped away. His hands strained upward, fingers reaching for the lip of the cliff; yet in that moment, the gravity of the void intensified, desperately seeking to claim him.

Thin arms materialized from mist -- reaching for him. Instinctually Greg seized the proffered wrists, as his rescuer solidified into view. It was a woman laying prone on the cliff edge. For an instant Greg was transfixed by her steady amber gaze. Her strained countenance was unfamiliar; yet Greg recognized that determined expression; the resiliency in her eyes. "Sage?!"

"Swing your legs!" The strain was obvious in her voice.

"I…can't." His arms were so tired!

"Try!"

With a groaning heave, Greg swung himself sideways, his foot smacking painfully against the cliff lip, just short of his target—the force of his motion threatening to drag Sage over the edge!

Her grip only intensified. "Again!"

Greg felt her beginning to slide! "But… you'll fall!"

"Do it!"

Using the momentum of the first swing - his tired stomach muscles knotting in agony - he threw up a leg; barely managing to hook his foot over the edge.

With Sage's assistance, Greg slowly wormed his way onto solid ground. Rolling away from the edge, he lay there_spent and gasping, unable to move. Her voice, strange yet familiar, spoke quietly as if fading away. "You've done it Greggory. It's almost over."

Chapter 11

Was it mere seconds, or an hour that he lay
upon the ledge? Time held no meaning.

Greg rolled over. His body felt so heavy! Every
movement took effort to complete. But at last -
dragging himself to his feet - he staggered off the
lip of stone and towards a cave far more grandiose
than this world's 'entryway'.

For set within the rock on its back wall, at the far
end of a brief corridor - complete with alcoves,
vaulted arches, and smooth grey pillars of
beautifully carved stone - shown a massive mirror,

bathed in the glow of a now strangely mottled sun—(warping as its solar energy was consumed by an infinity of starless night).

Greg stood directly in the path of light, yet no shadow was cast upon the glass. The light was piercing straight through him; his body becoming incorporeal. He had better get moving! "No rest for the wicked I see."

Yet… glancing at the mirrored alcove to his left, Greg was startled to see_in it stood a tall man, dressed in a red and brown striped tunic. His unusual square beard and ancient proud face, gave Greg pause.

Stepping closer, Greg watched as the still image faded away, replaced by an overhead view of this world's entryway. After a short pause, Greg's same agelessly youthful body stepped cautiously from the cave, walking on sandaled feet across the undisturbed gravel to examine the sign post, monogrammed with some long extinct script. Scanning his two options, he had quickly chosen the right hand path.

Confused, Greg trudged forward to the next alcove — another--shorter--man - dressed in an ancient leather skirt; another journey along the path—this time showing the steep slope just past the signpost, clear of rubble... and the thorn bushes - little more than small bristly sprouts.

The next mirror revealed a mongoloid man dressed in furs, followed by a scene at the stacks of boulders. Except, here they were not boulders, but a narrow passageway between towering cliffs; the walls riven with cracks, as if ready to crumble.

Each mirror he inspected, left Greg feeling more detached. Though gravity felt heavier, its effect on Greg was diminishing, his body slowly fading; yet there was more to it than that — each mirror revealed another man, another section along the path, rousing a niggling familiarity in Greg:

Here, a glimpse of wide meadow, grass trampled flat by many feet (surely an equivalent to the modern day football field); …There, a glimpse of that narrow climb of worldly gain; except here it was not so narrow and sheer—rather a gently rising berm. …And still further along, a wide dirt trek cutting through a massive tent city, harkening somehow to Greg's own middle years, raising his two youngest.

In each subsequent reflection, the damage to Greg's clothing and the path compounded, morphing into the final perilous trail Greg had traversed. Worst of all_was what had caused the destruction; for in every reflected journey_Greg witnessed the same occurrence; no less disturbing for its repetition:

A progressively less pallid man dragging his feet, sweat pouring down a face scorched red from the golden rays of a still vigorous sun rising in the far east, then - in later reflections - ascending to the sky's apex, even as his skin darkened from exposure. Why was there no water available along the path, as it had been when Greg became thirsty?

Inevitably a fogbank would arise, blocking off the narrow path. Seeming at first a welcome relief to the thirsty soul - the cool fog a moist balm to parched throat and blistered skin - he would stagger forward to be swallowed by the grey vapor …only to emerge moments later, fleeing whatever confrontation lurked within.

Despite his discouragement, Greg felt compelled to watch… and remember each journey that had ended in cowardice; pursued by the cloud until with a terrible lurch, the path would hurl him off - towards a distant, ethereal earth.

At last Greg came to a later mirror_where things were slightly different; the initial image that of a devoutly religious man – shoulders draped in a blue tasseled mantel. Water was provided along this journey, making it easier to progress. Nevertheless, sometime around midlife a fogbank arose, blocking the path.

Greg felt sure this man would successfully endure_and confront his offenses. Yet moments later he too fled from the cloud. Glancing over his shoulder in terror, the coward had voluntarily jumped off the path, and with a panicked cry, returned to mortality.

Stunned, Greg looked away from the mirror as the scene replayed. With his journey now successfully completed, he could only shake his

head at this long ago folly.

Each mirror examined left Greg with a personal

recollection of those events, as if it was he who had

lived them.

With a shiver Greg returned to the present,

noticing how weak the sun had become.

Hurriedly limping to the back of the cave, he

swiftly (and painfully) climbed five broad steps,

alighting on a semicircular dais of stone. Here

stood the thirteenth and final mirror.

As he approached, he spared only a swift glance

into the final side-mirrors, showcasing a diversity of men, widely varying in height, build, and skin color - the only thing they had in common; their near-identical expression of stern confidence.

Stepping up to the thirteenth mirror - his mirror - he thought back on all the mistakes Gregory Mason had made; the many wrongs he had visited upon those who had trusted him; depended on him. If this reflection was based solely on his wrongdoing – his, at times, blatant pride and deplorable self-interest – then this final reflection would be like all the others; that of a self-important, impeccably dressed man - the arrogance of pride stamped upon his face. Instead, reflected in the mirror was his current self, yet…well-rested in appearance—clothes fresh and new; identical to what Greg had worn on his first expedition.

Greg glanced down at his own dirty, scarred skin and ragged shorts, confused by the stark contrast in appearance. Coupled with that expression of inner peace - it seemed this idealized image of himself was a far kinder and more discerning man than Greg.

"Well, you're certainly different from all the others." His reflection gestured behind itself - mirroring his own movement - to the alcoves reflecting lifetimes of failure.

"I don't get it. What am I supposed to do? Please… tell me!" Greg's cry should have boomed loud in the vaulted hall, yet it retained that hollow, un-echoing quality from before—his words absorbed by the impinging vacuum. Odder yet, while Greg spoke, his reflected face remained unmoving; calm and peaceful, even as Greg's turned quizzical. "Why... hello, handsome!" Again there was no change of facial expression. Raising his arm, Greg waved it slowly back and forth, his twin mimicking the action.

Greg's jaw clenched in a growing panic. His body was becoming diaphanous, bordering on translucent! Yet the mirrored image bespoke a calm assurance.

Before Greg could reach forward to pound frantically on the glass, his reflection spoke indistinctly. Greg strained to hear, but caught only the faintest whisper. Then the reflection truly broke mirrorly conduct, raising its hand to earnestly beckon him forward; cupping its hands right up against the glass as Greg leaned forward.

"You're free to proceed," came the whisper in his ear. "Your debt has been paid by another. Step forward and become whole."

As the last rays of a blackened sun_set upon mortal time, a once prideful, then broken… and now truly humbled man - a shadow of his former self - pressed through the mirror, merging with this final reflection. Passing out of time, he now knew it was he who had been the reflection all along.

From outside the cave, the tall man nodded in satisfaction_before turning to face the oncoming void. Checking his watch, he too stepped out of existence.

Epilogue

Greg squinted his eyes; dazzled by intense sunlight off glistening stone, deflecting a mantled rainbow of brilliance — colors Greg had never seen before — could not have imagined. The sheer vibrancy of it should have pierced him, much as that sad dying sun had moments before; yet now he too was made of light, his whole body renewed – complete.

He felt - no sensed - a glorious strength and solidity to his being; all mortal imperfections consumed in the moment of melding with his true self. His once bared and bleeding feet - now shod in well-fitting sandals - stood sturdy and smooth; and his supple clothing_made of a natural fiber weave - felt snug against his clean, strong frame.

A hand slipped into his, warm and trusting—as a familiar arm slid around his back. How well he remembered the gentle feel of her at his side; she who had lifted him up from his last, and at long last, worthy life.

Looking down at her small, radiant figure – Greg marveled at her perfection; her slim form now a flawless reflection of her soul. Glancing away shyly, she looked out at a distant golden sun… just cresting the edge of this world; promising the start of a long and happy future. "It's glorious, isn't it?"

Greg just smiled and nodded his head.

ABOUT THE AUTHOR

Ammon Prolife is an organic farmer, moral activist, and avid science-fantasy reader. So it was only natural he took up writing what he loves.

Residing on his u-pick strawberry farm in Idaho with his hardworking family (and a surprisingly few number of animals), helps keep him grounded (and soiled), and gives him time to develop his new story ideas.

To find out more about those ideas, and how they are shaping up into books, visit his website:

www.ammonprolife.com